Sixty-Minute Shakespeare

Twelfth Night

by Cass Foster

Sixty-Minute Shakespeare

Twelfth Night

by Cass Foster

from TWELFTH NIGHT
by WILLIAM SHAKESPEARE

© Copyright 2003

published by
Five Star Publications, Inc.
Chandler, Arizona

SIXTY MINUTE SHAKESPEARE
TWELFTH NIGHT

by
Cass Foster

First Edition 1990. Second Edition 1997. Third Edition 1998.
Fourth Edition 2000. Fifth Edition 2001. Sixth Edition 2003.
All rights reserved. Printed in the United States of America.

Library of Congress Cataloging-in-Publication Data

Shakespeare, William, 1564-1616.
Twelfth Night / (abridged) by Cass Foster. — 1st ed.
    p.   cm. — (Classics for all ages) (The Sixty-Minute Shakespeare)
Summary: An abridged version of Shakespeare's comedy about love at first
sight, disguises, twins, and practical jokes.

ISBN: 1-877749-39-7

1. Survival after airplane accidents, shipwrecks, etc.—juvenile drama.
2. Brothers and sisters—Illyria—juvenile drama. 3. Twins—Illyria—juvenile
drama. 4. Children's plays. English
[1. Plays.] I. Shakespeare, William, 1564-1616.   Twelfth Night.
PS2837.A25 1997
822'. 914--dc21   97-28896
                                                                        CIP

Book Design by Barbara Kordesh
Paul M. Howey, Copy Editor
Sixth Edition edited by Gary E. Anderson

© 1990, 1997, 1998, 2000, 2001 and 2003 by Cass Foster

Five Star Publications, Incorporated
P.O. Box 6698
Chandler, AZ 85246-6698
website: www.FiveStarPublications.com/books/60MinuteShakespeare
e-mail: shakespeare@FiveStarPublications.com

To
Linda and Lowell

Welcome to
THE SIXTY-MINUTE SHAKESPEARE

Thanks to the progressive thinking of so many curriculum developers, Language Arts people and the splendid film work being done by directors such as Kenneth Branagh and Franco Zeffrelli, there has been a phenomenal growth in interest in Shakespeare.

No playwright, past or present, approaches the brilliance and magnitude of William Shakespeare. What other individual has even come close to understanding and then dramatizing the human condition? Just for the fun of it, I am listing (following these introductory remarks) a sample of themes and images so richly developed in the canon of his plays.

Shakespeare's characters are so well-rounded and beautifully constructed that it is common to see them as actual historical figures. When someone mentions Hamlet, Iago, Ophelia, or Puck, we immediately experience images and emotions that come from memories of people we know. We may feel compassion, frustration, sorrow, or pleasure.

As one of the wealthiest people of his times, Shakespeare earned his living as a playwright, theatre manager, actor, and shareholder in the Globe Theatre. He worked tirelessly to entertain. (Theatres presented a new play every day and the average new play had a total of only ten performances over an entire season.) He rebelled against the contemporary theatrical standards (the neo-classical principles that limited dramatic structure throughout France and Italy), he took plots from other published works (making them uniquely his own), and he created a spectacle (without the use of elaborate scenery) to captivate audiences of all social levels.

Imagine the challenge in quieting a crowd of three thousand in a theatre where vendors sell wine, beer, ale, nuts, and cards; where there is no intermission; where birds fly overhead; and where audience members stand near performers. Such was the setting in which Shakespeare's plays were originally staged.

The world's most familiar and successful wordsmith used language to skillfully create images, plot, and a sense of music and rhythm. The purpose behind this series is to reduce (not contemporize) the language. The unabridged Shakespeare simply isn't practical in all situations. Not all educators or directors have the luxury of time to explore the entire text. This is not intended to be a substitute for a thorough study of Shakespeare. It is merely a stepping stone.

I challenge each of you to go beyond the *Sixty-Minute* versions. Use the comfort, appreciation, and self-confidence you will gain to go further. Be proud of the insights and knowledge you acquire, but do not be satisfied. The more you read, the more you gain.

May each of you be blessed with an abundance of good health and happiness. I thank you for your interest in our work and hope you are pleased with what we have done.

May the Verse Be With You!

A COUPLE OF STAGING CONSIDERATIONS

Scenery

There are two excellent reasons theatres rarely use much scenery when staging Shakespeare. The first is related to the number of changes required. If we have to wait every five to ten minutes to watch scenery struck and set up, we end up watching a play about moving lumber. The second is because the audience will lose sight of what the play is about. Audiences need a couple minutes to adjust to the new scenic look of a dazzling waterfall and lush forest. By the time they take it all in and start paying attention to what the actors are saying, it is time to set up the next scene and the audience will be lost.

Location is normally established through dialogue and the use of a few simple props: a throne-like chair for the king's court, a long table with benches for an inn, or a bed for the queen's bed chamber. The key is to keep it simple.

Pacing

You will want to keep things moving all the time. That doesn't mean actors should talk and move quickly; it simply means one scene should flow smoothly to the next without delay or interruption.

As Scene One ends, the actors pick up their props and walk off. Actors for Scene Two enter from a different direction with their props and begin dialogue as soon as they enter the acting area, putting their props in place as they speak. Yes, the audience will still have view of the actors in the first scene, but they will gladly accept this convention if it means taking fifteen minutes off performance time.

TWO HIGHLY RECOMMENDED WEB SITES

www.ShakeSpirit.com

A revolutionary site offering Shakespeare gifts,
teaching assistance, resources and quotes.

www.ShakespeareLRC.com

SHAKESPEARE LEARNING RESOURCE CENTER.
Free Library Dedicated to Shakespeare
and the Performing and Visual Arts.

IMAGES AND THEMES TO LOOK FOR
IN THE VARIOUS PLAYS

Mistaken identity	Foils or opposites
Wisdom of fools	Spying
Insanity	Paranoia
Greed and corruption	Play-acting
Religious persecution	Justice
The elements	Heavenly retribution
The supernatural	Forgiveness
Darkness and light	Witchcraft
Loneliness or isolation	Mortality
Anti-Semitism	Self-destruction
Conspiracy	Black or white magic
Revenge	Animals
Hypocrisy	Nature
Abandonment	Reality vs. illusion
Pride	Astrological influence
Honor	Characters reforming
Violence	Old age
Bravery	Freedom
Rebellion	Usurping of power
Savagery	Fertility suppression
Seduction	Sexual misadventure
Disease or physical decay	Melancholy
Loyalty	Corrupt society
War	Love and/or friendship
Marriage	Multiple meanings of words
False accusations	Thought vs. action
Irresponsible power	Impetuous love
Destiny or fate	Role of women
Real or pretended madness	Human frailty
Ambition	Preparing for leadership
Tyranny	Charity/Betrayal

THE COMPLETE WORKS
OF WILLIAM SHAKESPEARE

1589 - 1591	Henry VI, Part 1, 2 and 3
1592 - 1593	Richard III
1593 - 1594	Titus Andronicus
1592 - 1594	Comedy of Errors
1593 - 1594	Taming of the Shrew
1594	The Two Gentlemen of Verona
1594 - 1595	Love's Labor's Lost
1594 - 1596	King John
1595	Richard II
1595 - 1596	A Midsummer Night's Dream
1595 - 1596	Romeo and Juliet
1596 - 1597	The Merchant of Venice
1597	The Merry Wives of Windsor
1597 - 1598	Henry IV, Part 1 and 2
1598 - 1599	Much Ado About Nothing
1599	Henry V
1599	Julius Caesar
1599	As You Like It
1600 - 1601	Hamlet
1601 - 1602	Twelfth Night
1601 - 1602	Troilus and Cressida
1602 - 1603	All's Well That Ends Well
1604	Measure for Measure
1604	Othello
1605	The Tragedy of King Lear
1606	Macbeth
1606 - 1607	Antony and Cleopatra
1607 - 1608	Timon of Athens
1607 - 1608	Pericles, Prince of Tyre
1607 - 1608	Coriolanus
1609- 1610	Cymbeline
1609 - 1610	The Winter's Tale
1611	The Tempest
1612 - 1613	Henry VIII
1613	Two Noble Kinsmen (Authorship in question)

23 April 1564 - 23 April 1616

" *If we wish to know the force of human genius,*
we should read Shakespeare. If we wish to see the
insignificance of human learning, we may study
his commentators."

William Hazlitt (1778-1830) English Essayist. "On the Ignorance of the
Learned," in *Edinburgh Magazine* (July 1818).

COMMON QUOTES FROM THE BARD

Romeo and Juliet

Parting is such sweet sorrow.
A plague o' both your houses.
O Romeo, Romeo! Wherefore art thou Romeo?

A Midsummer Night's Dream

Lord, what fools these mortals be.
The course of true love never did run smooth.
To say the truth, reason and love keep little company
together now-a-days.

As You Like It

All that glisters is not gold.
Love is blind.
All the world's a stage
And all the men and women merely players.
For ever and a day.

Twelfth Night

Some are born great, some achieve greatness, and some
have greatness thrust upon them.
Out of the jaws of death.
O, had I but followed the arts!
Many a good hanging prevents a bad marriage.

Henry IV, Part 1

The better part of valor is discretion.
To give the devil his due.
He hath eaten me out of house and home.

Henry VI, Part 2

Let's kill all the lawyers.

The Merry Wives of Windsor

Better three hours too soon than a minute too late.

Casablanca

This could be the start of a beautiful friendship.

Macbeth

> Out, damned spot. Out, I say!
> Screw your courage to the sticking place.

Hamlet

> Something is rotten in the state of Denmark.
> To be or not to be. That is the question.
> The lady doth protest too much, methinks.
> Good night, sweet prince, And flights of
>   angels sing thee to thy rest!

The Merchant of Venice

> The devil can cite scriptures for his purpose.

Pericles

> Few love to hear the sins they love to act.

Richard III

> Now is the winter of our discontent.
> Off with his head!
> A horse! A horse! My kingdom for a horse.

Julius Caesar

> Beware the ides of March.
> Friends, Romans, countrymen, lend me your ears.
> It was Greek to me.

Much Ado About Nothing

> The world must be peopled. When I said I would die a
>   bachelor, I did not think I should live till I were married.

Measure for Measure

> The miserable have no other medicine but only hope.

Troilus and Cressida

> To fear the worst oft cures the worse.

The Comedy of Errors

> Unquiet meals make ill digestions.

Cast of Characters

Orsino, Duke of Illyria
Valentine, gentleman attending the Duke
Curio, gentleman attending the Duke

Viola, sister of Sebastian
Sea Captain, friend to Viola
Sebastian, brother of Viola
Antonio, a sea captain, friend to Sebastian

Olivia, a countess
Sir Toby Belch, uncle to Olivia
Malvolio, steward to Olivia
Fabian, servant to Olivia
Feste, a clown, servant to Olivia
Maria, Olivia's woman
Sir Andrew Aguecheek

Lords, Priest, Two Officers, Musicians and Attendants.

Place
Illyria

ACT I, SCENE 1.
PALACE OF DUKE ORSINO

Enter Orsino, Curio, Lords, and Musicians.

Duke. If music be the food of love, play on.
  Give me excess of it, that, ~~surfeiting~~, *excess*
  The appetite may sicken, and so die.
  ~~That strain again. It had a dying fall°.~~
  ~~O, it came o'er my ear like the sweet sound~~
  ~~That breathes upon a bank of violets,~~
  ~~Stealing and giving odor.~~ Enough, no more.
  'Tis not so sweet now as it was before.

Curio. Will you go hunt, my lord?

Duke. What, Curio?

Curio. The ~~hart.~~ *deer.*

Duke. Why, so I do, the noblest that I have. O, when mine
  eyes did see Olivia first, methought she purged the air of
  pestilence. That instant was I turned into a hart.

Enter Valentine.

Duke. How now? What news from her?

Valentine. So please my lord, I might not be admitted,
  But from her handmaid do return this answer:
  ~~The element° itself, till seven years' heat°,~~ *Her face remains covered*
  ~~Shall not behold her face at ample view;~~

Fall: cadence.   *Element:* sky.   Heat: course.

1

[Valentine.]   ~~All this to season~~ *All this to outvie honour*
    A brother's dead love, which she would keep
    Fresh and lasting in her sad remembrance.

Duke. O, she that hath a heart of that fine frame
    To pay this debt of love but to a brother,
    How will she love when the rich golden ~~shaft~~ *of Cupid*
    ~~Hath killed the flock of all affections else°~~ *kills all other*
    ~~That live in her.~~ Away before me to sweet beds of flow'rs; *affections*
    ~~Love thoughts lie rich when canopied with bow'rs.~~

They exit.

ACT I, SCENE 2.
THE SEACOAST OF ILLYRIA.

Enter Viola and Captain. [Sailors optional.]

Viola. What country, friend, is this?

Captain. This is Illyria, lady.

Viola. And what should I do in Illyria?
    My brother he is in Elysium°.
    Perchance he is not drowned. What think you?

Captain. It is perchance that you yourself were saved.
    When you, and those poor number saved with you,
    Hung on our driving° boat, I saw your brother,
    ~~Most provident in peril,~~ bind himself

When...else: i.e. when Cupid's arrow has slain all emotions except love.   *Elysium:*
heaven.   *Driving:* drifting.

2

[Captain.] To a strong mast that lived° upon the sea;
  Where, like Arion° on the dolphin's back,
  I saw him hold acquaintance with the waves
  So long as I could see.

Viola. For saying so, there's gold.
  Know'st thou this country?

Captain. Aye, madam, well, for I was bred and born
  Not three hours' travel from this very place.

Viola. Who governs here?

Captain. A noble duke, in nature as in name.

Viola. What is his name?

Captain. Orsino.

Viola. Orsino! I have heard my father name him.
  He was a bachelor then.

Captain. And so is now, or was so very late;
  For he did seek the love of fair Olivia.

Viola. What's she?

Captain. A virtuous maid, the daughter of a count
  That died some twelvemonth since, then leaving her
  In the protection of his son, her brother,

Lived: floated.   *Arion:* Greek poet who escaped murderous sailors by leaping
overboard to be rescued by dolphins

[Captain.] Who shortly also died; for whose dear love,
    They say, she hath ~~abjured~~ the company *[swarn off]*
    And sight of men. ~~She will admit no kind of suit,~~
    ~~No, not the Duke's~~

Viola. I prithee, conceal me what I am.
    I'll serve the duke.
    Thou shalt present me as ~~an eunuch°~~ *a soprano* to him;
    ~~It may be worth thy pains.~~ For I can sing, *and be worthyor*
    ~~And speak to him in many sorts of music~~ *his servise*
    That will allow me ~~very~~ worth his service.
    What else may hap, to time I will commit;
    Only shape thou thy silence to my wit.

Captain. Be you his eunuch, *[soprano]* and your mute I'll be;
    When my tongue blabs, then let mine eyes not see.

Viola. I thank thee. Lead me on.

They exit.

Eunuch: a castrato or male soprano singer. Her high-pitched voice will allow her to pass as a male. She actually becomes his page.

Please note:
Not everyone realizes it is not only illegal to photocopy copyrighted material but by photocopying (and reducing sales) small publishing houses like ours will not be able to generate sufficient resources to create additional works. We appreciate your understanding and assistance.

ACT I, SCENE 3.
OLIVIA'S HOUSE.

Enter Sir Toby and Maria.

Toby. What a plague means my niece to take the death
of her brother thus?

Maria. By my troth, Sir Toby, you must come in earlier
o' nights. Your cousin°, my lady, takes great
exceptions to your ill hours. You must confine
yourself within the modest limits of order.

Toby. Confine? I'll confine myself no finer than I am.
These clothes are good enough to drink in, and so be
these boots too.

Maria. That quaffing and drinking will undo you°. I
heard my lady talk of it yesterday; and of a foolish knight
that you brought in one night here to be her wooer.

Toby. Who? Sir Andrew Aguecheek°?

Maria. Aye, he.

Toby. He's as tall man as any's in Illyria.

Maria. What's that to th' purpose?

Cousin. kinsman.   *Undo you:* be the ruin of you.   *Aguecheek:* suggesting a thin,
pale face like that of a man with ague.

Toby. Why, he has three thousand ducats° a year.

Maria. Aye, he'll have but a year in all these ducats°.
He's a very fool and a prodigal. He's drunk nightly.

Toby. With drinking healths to my niece. I'll drink to her as
long as there is a passage in my throat and drink in
Illyria. He's a coward and a coystrill° that will not drink
to my niece—Ah, here comes Sir Andrew Agueface°.

Enter Sir Andrew.

Andrew. Sir Toby Belch. How now, Sir Toby Belch?

Toby. Sweet Sir Andrew.

Andrew. Bless you, fair shrew.

Maria. And you too, sir.

Toby. Accost, Sir Andrew, accost°.

Andrew. What's that?

Toby. My niece's chambermaid°.

Andrew. Good Mistress Accost, I desire better acquaintance.

Ducats: gold coin.   *He'll...ducats:* he'll run through his estate in a year.   *Coystrill:*
knave.   *Agueface:* possibly a mistake and eventually kept in the text as a jest.
Accost: talk to her.   *Chambermaid:* like a lady in waiting. (Not of low social sta-
tus in this household.)

Maria. My name is Mary, sir.

Andrew. Good Mistress Mary Accost.

Toby. You mistake, knight. 'Accost' is front her°,
   board her, woo her, assail her.

Andrew. By my troth, I would not undertake her in this
   company. Is that the meaning of 'accost?'

Maria. Fare you well, gentlemen.

She exits.

Toby. O knight, thou lack'st a cup of ~~canary°!~~ wine

Sir Toby hands Sir Andrew a cup of wine.

Andrew. Methinks sometimes I have no more wit than
   a Christian or an ordinary man has. But I am a greater
   eater of beef, and I believe that does harm to my wit.

Toby. No question.

Andrew. An I thought that, I'd forswear it. I'll ride home
   tomorrow, Sir Toby. Your niece will not be seen by me.
   The Count himself here hard by woos her.

Front her: board her.   *Canary:* sweet wine from the Canary Islands.

Toby. She'll none of the Count. I have heard her swear't. Tut, there's life in't man.

Andrew. I'll stay a month longer. I am a fellow o' th' *of the* strangest mind in th' world. I delight in masques and revels sometimes altogether.

Toby. What is thy excellence in a galliard°, knight?

Andrew. Faith, I can cut a caper°.

Toby. I think, by the excellent constitution of thy leg, it was formed under the star of a galliard.

Andrew. Aye, 'tis strong, and it does indifferent well in a dun-colored stock. Shall we set about some revels?

Toby. What shall we do else? Were we not born under Taurus°?

Andrew. Taurus? That's sides and hearts.

Toby. No, sir, it is legs and thighs. Let me see thee caper. Ha, higher! Ha, ha, excellent!

Andrew continues to leap as they exit.

Galliard: quick dance in triple time.   *Cut a caper:* execute a leap.   *Taurus:* a zodiac sign that controls neck and throat. (Here suggested it also controls "legs and thighs.")

ACT I, SCENE 4.
THE PALACE OF DUKE ORSINO.

Enter Valentine, and Viola who is dressed in man's attire.

Valentine. If the Duke continues these favors toward you,
Cesario, you are like to be much advanced. He hath
known you but three days and already you are no
stranger.

Enter Duke, Curio and Attendants.

Viola. Here comes the Count.

Duke. Who saw Cesario, ho?

Viola. On your attendance, my lord, here.

Duke. Stand you awhile aloof. *[All but Viola exit.]*
　Cesario, good youth, address thy gait° unto her;
　Be not denied access, stand at her doors, And tell them
　there thy fixed foot shall grow till thou have audience.

Viola.   Sure, my noble lord.
　Say I do speak with her, my lord, what then?

Duke. O, then unfold the passion of my love.
　She will attend it better in thy youth
　Then in a nuncio's° of more grave aspect.

Address thy gait. direct your steps.   *Nuncio's:* messenger's.

9

Viola. I think not so, my lord.

Duke.   Diana's lip
   Is not more smooth and rubious°; thy small pipe°
   Is as the maiden's organ, shrill and sound°,
   And all is semblative° a woman's part.
                              Prosper well in this,
   And thou shalt live as freely as thy lord
   To call his fortunes thine.

Viola.   I'll do my best to woo your lady. *[Aside.]* Yet a
   barful strife°! Whoe'er I woo, myself would be his wife.

They exit.

ACT I, SCENE 5.
OLIVIA'S HOUSE.

Enter Maria and Clown.

Clown. Let her hang me. He that is well hanged in this
   world needs to fear no colors°.

Maria. You will be hanged for being so long absent.

Clown. Many a good hanging prevents a bad marriage.

Maria. Peace, you rogue. Here comes my lady.

Enter Olivia.

Rubious: ruby red.   *Small pipe:* throat.   *Shrill and sound:* high and clear.
Semblative: like.   *Barful strife:* a conflict with (for me) serious impediments.
Fear no colors: fear nothing.

10

Olivia. Take the fool away.

Clown. Do you not hear, fellows? Take away the lady.

Olivia. Go to, y' are a dry fool.

Clown. Good madonna°, give me leave to prove you a fool.

Olivia. Can you do it?

Clown. Dexteriously.

Olivia. Make your proof.

Clown. Good madonna, why mourn'st thou?

Olivia. Good fool, for my brother's death.

Clown. I think his soul is in hell, madonna.

Olivia. I know his soul is in heaven, fool.

Clown. The more fool, madonna, to mourn for your brother's soul, being in heaven. Take away the fool, gentlemen.

Clown exits laughing. Enter Malvolio.

Malvolio. Madam, there is at the gate a young gentleman
much desires to speak with you. I told him you were sick;
he takes on him to understand so much, and therefore

Madonna: my lady.

[Malvolio.] comes to speak with you. I told him you were
   asleep; he seems to have a foreknowledge of that too, and
   therefore comes to speak with you. What is to be said of
   him, lady?

Olivia. What kind of man is he?

Malvolio. Why, of mankind.

Olivia. What manner of man?

Malvolio. Of very ill manner.

Olivia. Of what personage and years is he?

Malvolio. Not yet old enough for a man nor young enough
   for a boy. One would think his mother's milk were scarce
   out of him.

Olivia. Let him approach. *[To Maria.]*
   Give me my veil; come, throw it o'er my face.
   We'll once more hear Orsino's embassy.

Enter Viola.

Viola. The honorable lady of the house, which is she?

Olivia. Speak to me; I shall answer for her. Your will?

Viola. Most radiant, exquisite, and unmatchable beauty...
   I pray you tell me if this be the lady of the house, for I
   never saw her. I would be loath to cast away my speech;
   for, besides that it is excellently well penned, I have taken
   great pains to con it.

Olivia. Are you a comedian?

Viola. No, my profound heart; and yet I am not that I play.
Are you the lady of the house?

Olivia. If I do not usurp myself, I am.

Viola. ~~This is from my commission.~~ I will on with my
speech in your praise and then show you the heart of my
message.

Olivia. Come to what is important in't. I forgive you the
praise.

Viola. Alas, I took great pain to study it, and 'tis poetical.

Olivia. It is more like to be feigned; I pray you keep it in. If
you be not mad, be gone; if you have reason, be brief.

Maria. Will you hoist sail, sir? Here lies your way.

Viola. No, good swabber°; I am to hull° here a little longer.

Olivia. Sure you have some hideous matter to deliver.
Speak your office.

Viola. It alone concerns your ear. My words are as full of
peace as matter.

Olivia. Give us the place alone; we will hear this divinity°.

[Maria exits.]

Swabber: one who washes decks.   *Hull:* float without sail.   *Divinity:* holy message.

Olivia. Now, sir, what is your text?

Viola. Most sweet lady.

Olivia. A comfortable doctrine, and much may be said of it. Where lies your text?

Viola. In Orsino's bosom.

Olivia. In his bosom? In what chapter of his bosom?

Viola. To answer by the method, in the first of his heart.

Olivia. O, I have read it; it is heresy. Have you no more to say?

Viola. Good madam, let me see your face.

Olivia. Have you any commission from your lord to negotiate with my face? You are now out of your text. But we will draw the curtain and show you the picture. *[Unveils.]* Look you, sir, such a one I was this present°. Is't not well done?

Viola. Exceedingly done, if G-d° did all.

Olivia. 'Tis in grain, sir; 'twill endure wind and weather.

Viola. 'Tis beauty truly bent, whose red and white Nature's own sweet and cunning° hand laid on.

This present: a minute ago.   *Cunning:* skillful.

[Viola.] Lady, you are the cruel'st she alive
   If you will lead these graces to the grave,
   And leave the world no copy.

Olivia. O, sir, I will not be so hard-hearted. I will give out
   divers schedules° of my beauty. It shall be inventoried,
   and every particle and utensil° labeled to my will; as,
   item, two lips, indifferent red; item, two grey eyes, with
   lids to them; item, one neck, one chin, and so forth…
   Were you sent hither to praise me?

Viola. I see what you are, you are too proud;
   But if you were the devil, you are fair.
   My lord and master loves you.

Olivia. Your lord does know my mind; I cannot love him.
   Yet I suppose him virtuous, know him noble,
   Of great estate, of fresh and stainless youth;
   A gracious person. But yet I cannot love him.
   He might have took his answer long ago.

Viola. If I did love you in my master's flame,
   With such a suff'ring, such a deadly° life,
   In your denial I would find no sense;
   I would not understand it.

Olivia.   Why, what would you?

Viola. Make me a willow° cabin at your gate
   And call upon my soul within the house;

Divers schedules: itemized lists.   *Utensil.* article.   *Deadly:* death-like.   *Willow:*
symbol of grief for unrequited love.

[Viola.] Write loyal cantons° of contemned° love
  And sing them loud even in the dead of night.

Olivia. You might do much. What is your parentage?

Viola. Above my fortunes, yet my state is well.
  I am a gentleman.

Olivia.   Get you to your lord.
  I cannot love him. Let him send no more,
  Unless, perchance, you come to see me again
  To tell me how he takes it. Fare you well.
  I thank you for your pains. Spend this for me.

Viola. I am no fee'd post°, lady; keep your purse;
  My master, not myself, lacks recompense.
  Farewell, fair cruelty.

She exits.

Olivia. 'What is your parentage?'
  'Above my fortunes, yet my state is well.
  I am a gentleman.' I'll be sworn thou art.
  Thy tongue, thy face, thy limbs, actions, and spirit
  Do give thee fivefold blazon°. Not too fast, soft°, soft.
  How now? Even so quickly may one catch the plague?
  Well, let it be. . .What ho, Malvolio!

Enter Malvolio.

Malvolio. Here, madam, at your service.

Cantons: songs. *Contemnéd:* rejected. *Fee'd post:* messenger to be tipped.
Blazon: coat of arms. *Soft:* stay.

Olivia. Run after that same peevish messenger.
  He left this ring behind him. Tell him I'll none of it.
  ~~Desire him not to flatter with~~ his lord
  ~~Nor hold him up with hopes.~~
  If that the youth will come this way tomorrow,
  I'll give him reasons for't. Hie thee, Malvolio.

Malvolio. Madam, I will. [He exits.]

Olivia. I do not know what, and fear to find
  Mine eye too great a flatterer for my mind.
  Fate, show thy force; ourselves we do not owe.
  What is decreed must be…and be this so!

ACT II, SCENE 1.
THE SEACOAST.

Enter Antonio and Sebastian.

Sebastian. No. My stars shine darkly over me; the
malignancy° of my fate might perhaps distemper yours.
Therefore I shall crave of you your leave, that I may bear
my evils alone.

Antonio. Let me know of you whither you are bound.

Sebastian. My determinate° voyage is mere extravagancy°.
Antonio, my name is Sebastian, which I called Roderigo.
My father was that Sebastian of Messaline° whom I know
you have heard of. He left behind him myself and a sister,
both born in an hour. If the heavens had been pleased,
would we had so ended! But you, sir, altered that, for
some hour before you took me from the beach of the sea
was my sister drowned.

Antonio. Alas the day!

Sebastian. A lady, sir, though it was said she much resem-
bled me. She drowned already, sir, with salt water, though
I seem to drown her remembrance again with more.

Owe: own.   *Malignancy:* evilness or deadliness.   *Determinate:* intended.
Extravagancy: wandering.   *Messaline:* possibly in Sicily.

Antonio. Pardon me, sir, your bad entertainment°.

Sebastian. O good Antonio, forgive me your trouble.

Antonio. Let me be your servant.

Sebastian. If you will not undo what you have done, that is,
kill him whom you have recovered, desire it not. Fare ye
well at once. My bosom is full of kindness, and I am yet
so near the manners of my mother that, upon the least
occasion more, mine eyes will tell tales of me. I am
bound to the Count Orsino's court. Farewell.

He exits.

Antonio. The gentleness of all the gods go with thee. I have
many enemies in Orsino's court, else would I very shortly
see thee there. But come what may, I do adore thee so
That danger shall seem sport, and I will go. *[He exits.]*

Your bad entertainment: for not speaking of subjects more appropriate to one's
guest.

ACT II, SCENE 2.
STREET NEAR OLIVIA'S HOUSE.

Enter Viola and Malvolio, who quickly catches up to her.

Malvolio. Were not you ev'n now with the Countess Olivia?

Viola. Even now, sir. On a moderate pace I have since arrived but hither.

Malvolio. She returns this ring to you, sir. You might have saved me my pains, to have taken it away yourself. She adds, moreover, that you should put your lord into a desperate assurance° she will none of him.

Viola. She took the ring of me. I'll none of it.

Malvolio. Come, sir, you peevishly threw it to her, and her will is, it should be so returned. If it be worth stooping for, there it lies, in your eye; if not, be it his that finds it.

He exits.

Viola. I left no ring with her. What means this lady?
Fortune forbid my outside have not charmed her...
She loves me sure; the cunning° of her passion
Invites me in this churlish messenger.
Poor lady, she were better love a dream...
And I poor monster° fond as much on him;
And she, mistaken, seems to dote on me.
What will become of this? As I am man,
My master loves her dearly;

Desperate assurance: certainty without hope.   *Cunning:* craftiness.   *Monster:* i.e. being both a man and a woman.

[Viola.] My state is desperate° for my master's love.
　　As I am woman—now alas the day!—
　　What thriftless° sighs shall poor Olivia breathe?
　　O Time, thou must untangle this, not I;
　　It is too hard a knot for me t' untie.

She exits.

ACT II, SCENE 3.
OLIVIA'S HOUSE.

Enter Sir Toby and Sir Andrew.

Toby. Approach, Sir Andrew. Not to be abed after midnight
　　is to be up betimes°.

Andrew. I know to be up late is to be up late.

Toby. Thou art a scholar! Let us therefore eat and drink.
　　Marian, I say! A stoop° of wine!

Enter Clown.

Andrew. Here comes the fool, in faith.

Clown. How now, my hearts°.

Toby. Come! There is sixpence for you. Let's have a song.

Clown. Would you have a love song, or a song of good life°?

Toby. A love song, a love song.

Desperate. hopeless.　*Thriftless:* unprofitable.　*Betimes:* in good season.　*Stoop:*
goblet.　*Hearts:* a term of endearment.　*Good life·* virtuous living.

Andrew. Aye, aye, I care not for good life.

Clown. [Singing.]
>O mistress mine, where are you roaming?
>O, stay and hear! Your truelove's coming,
>   That can sing both high and low.
>Trip no further, pretty sweeting;
>Journeys end in lovers meeting,
>   Every wise man's son doth know.

Andrew. Excellent good, in faith.

Toby. Good, good.

Andrew. A mellifluous voice, as I am a true knight.

Toby. To hear by the nose, it is dulcet in contagion°. But shall we make the welkin° dance indeed? Shall we rouse the night owl in a catch that will draw three souls out of one weaver? Shall we do that?

Andrew. An you love me, let's do't. I am dog at a catch.

Clown. By'r Lady, sir, and some dogs will catch well.

Andrew. Begin, fool. It begins, 'Hold thy peace.'

Clown. I shall never begin if I hold my peace.

Andrew. Good, in faith! Come, begin.

Clown begins to play as Maria enters.

To... contagion: if we could hear by the nose we could call it sweetly stinking.
Welkin: sky.

24

Maria. What a caterwauling do you keep here? If my lady
   have not called up her steward Malvolio and bid him
   turn you out of doors, never trust me.

Toby. Am I not consanguineous°? Am I not of her blood?
   Tilly-vally°, lady. *[Sings.]* 'There dwelt a man in Babylon,
   lady, lady.'

Clown. Beshrew me, the knight's in admirable fooling.

Andrew. Aye, he does well enough if he be disposed, and so
   do I too. He does it with a better grace, but I do it more
   natural.

Maria. For the love o' G-d, peace!

Enter Malvolio.

Malvolio. My masters, are you mad? Or what are you?
   Have you no wit, manners, nor honesty, but to gabble
   like tinkers at this time of night? Is there no respect for
   place, persons, nor time in you?

Toby. We did keep time, sir, in our catches. Sneck up°.

Malvolio. Sir Toby. My lady bade me tell you that, though
   she harbors you as her kinsman, she's nothing allied to
   your disorders. If you can separate yourself and your
   misdemeanors, you are welcome to the house. If not,
   and it would please you to take leave of her, she is very
   willing to bid you farewell.

Consanguineous: related.   *Tilly-vally:* nonsense.   *Sneck up:* go hang yourself.

Toby. *[Sings.]* 'Farewell, dear heart, since I must needs be gone.'

Maria. Nay, good Sir Toby.

Clown. *[Sings.]* 'His eyes do show his days are almost done.'

Toby. *[Sings.]* 'But I never will die.'

Clown. *[Sings.]* 'Sir Toby, there you lie.'

Toby. A stoop of wine, Maria!

Malvolio. Mistress Mary, if you prized my lady's favor at anything more than contempt, you would not give means for this uncivil rule. She shall know of it, by this hand.

[He exits.]

Maria. Go shake your ears.

Andrew. 'Twere as good a deed as to drink when a man's ahungry, to challenge him the field, and then to break promise with him and make a fool of him.

Toby. Do't, knight. I'll write thee a challenge; or I'll deliver thy indignation to him by word of mouth.

Maria. And on that vice in him will my revenge find notable cause to work.

Toby. What wilt thou do?

Maria. I will drop in his way some obscure epistles of love, wherein by the color of his beard, the shape of his leg,

[Maria.] the manner of his gait, the expressure° of his eye, forehead, and complexion, he shall find himself most feelingly personated. I can write very like my lady your niece.

Toby. Excellent. I smell a device.

Andrew. I have't in my nose too.

Toby. He shall drink by the letters that thou wilt drop that they come from my niece, and that she's in love with him.

Maria. I will plant you two, and let the fool make a third, where he shall find the letter. Observe his construction° of it. For this night, to bed, and dream on the event. Farewell.

She exits.

Toby. She's a beagle true-bred, and one that adores me. What o' that?

Andrew. I was adored once too.

Toby. Let's to bed, knight. Thou hadst need send for more money.

Andrew. If I cannot recover your niece, I am a foul way out°.

Toby. Send for money, knight. If thou hast her not in th' end, call me Cut°.

Andrew. If I do not, never trust me, take it how you will.

Expressure: expression.   *Construction* interpretation.   *A foul way out:* practically bankrupt.   *Cut:* horse with a docked tail.

Toby. Come, come; I'll go burn some sack°. 'Tis too late to
   go to bed now. Come, knight, come, knight.

They exit.

ACT II, SCENE 4.
ORSINO'S PALACE.

Enter Duke, Viola, Curio, and others.

Duke. Give me some music. Now, good morrow, friends.
   Now, good Cesario, but that piece of song,
   That old and antique song we heard last night.
   Methought it did relieve my passion much.
   Come, but one verse.

Curio. He is not here, so please your lordship, that should
   sing it.

Duke. Who was it?

Curio. Feste the jester, my lord. He is about the house.

Duke. Seek him out, and play the tune the while.

Exit Curio as music plays.

Duke. Come hither, boy. How dost thou like this tune?

Viola. It gives a very echo to the seat
   Where Love is throned.

Burn some sack: warm some sherry.

Duke.   ˙ Thou dost speak masterly.
  My life upon't, young though thou art, thine eye
  Hath stayed upon some favor that it loves.
  Hath it not, boy?

Viola.   A little, by your favor.

Duke. What kind of woman is it?

Viola.   Of your complexion.

Duke. She is not worth thee then. What years, in faith?

Viola. About your years, my lord.

Duke. Too old, by heaven.
  Let thy love be younger than thyself,
  Or thy affection cannot hold the bent;
  For woman are as roses, whose fair flow'r,
  Being once displayed, doth fall that very hour.

Viola. And so they are; alas, that they are so.
  To die, even when they to perfection grow.

Enter Curio and Clown.

Duke. O, fellow, come, the song we had last night.
  Mark it, Cesario; it is old and plain.
  It dallies with the innocence of love,
  Like the old age°.

Old age: good ol' days.

29

Clown. Are you ready, sir?

Duke. I prithee, sing.

Music begins.

Clown. [Sings.]

> Come away, come away, death,
>   And in sad cypress let me be laid.
> Fly away, fly away, breath;
>   I am slain by a fair cruel maid.
> My shroud of white, stuck all with yew,
>   O, prepare it.
> My part of death, no one so true
>   Did share it.

Duke. There's for thy pains.

Clown. No pains, sir. I take pleasure in singing, sir.

Duke. I'll pay thy pleasure then. *[Pays him.]* Give me now leave to leave thee.

Clown. Now the melancholy god protect thee, and the tailor make thy doublet° of changeable taffeta°, for thy mind is very opal. Farewell. *[He exits.]*

Duke. Let all the rest give place.

All but the Duke and Viola exit.

Doublet: close-fitting jacket.   *Changeable taffeta:* silken material where color changes with movement.

Duke.   Once more, Cesario,
  Get thee to yond same sovereign cruelty.
  Tell her, my love, more noble than the world,
  Prizes not quantity of dirty lands;
  The parts° that fortune hath bestowed upon her
  Tell her I hold as giddily as fortune.

Viola. But if she cannot love you, sir?

Duke. I cannot be so answered.

Viola.   Sooth, but you must.
  Say that some lady, as perhaps there is,
  Hath for your love as great a pang of heart
  As you have for Olivia. You cannot love her.
  You tell her so. Must she not then be answered?

Duke.   Make no compare
  Between that love a woman can bear me
  And that I owe Olivia.

Viola.   Aye, but I know.

Duke. What dost thou know?

Viola. Too well what love women to men may owe.
  In faith, they are as true of heart as we.
  My father had a daughter loved a man
  As it might be perhaps, were I a woman,
  I should your lordship.

Parts: possessions.

31

Duke.   And what's her history?

Viola. A blank, my lord. She never told her love,
   But let concealment, like a worm in th' bud,
   Feed on her damask° cheek. She pined in thought;
   And, with a green and yellow melancholy,
   She sat like patience on a monument, smiling at grief.

Duke. But died thy sister of her love, my boy?

Viola. I am all the daughters of my father's house,
   And all the brothers too, and yet I know not.
   Sir, shall I to this lady?

Duke.   Aye, that's the theme.
   To her in haste. Give her this jewel. Say
   My love can give no place, bide no denay°.

They exit.

ACT II, SCENE 5.
OLIVIA'S GARDEN.

Enter Maria, Sir Toby, Sir Andrew, and Fabian.

Maria. Malvolio's coming down this walk. Observe him,
   for the love of mockery; for I know this letter will make a
   contemplative idiot of him. Close, in the name of jesting!
   [The men hide themselves.] Lie thou there, *[Throws down
   the letter.]* for here comes the trout that must be caught
   with tickling. *[She exits as Malvolio enters.]*

Damask: pink and white, as a damask rose.   *Denay:* denial.

32

Malvolio. 'Tis but fortune; all is fortune. Maria once told me she did affect me°; and I have heard herself come thus near, that, should she fancy, it should be one of my complexion°. What should I think on't?

Toby. Here's an overweening rogue.

Andrew. 'Slight°, I could so beat that rogue.

Toby. Peace, I say.

Malvolio. To be Count Malvolio.

Toby. Ah, rogue!

Andrew. Pistol him, pistol him.

Malvolio. Having been three months married to her, calling my officers about me, in my branched velvet gown; having come from a day bed, where I have left Olivia sleeping.

Toby. Fire and brimstone!

Fabian. O, peace, peace!

Malvolio. What employment° have we here?

He picks up the letter.

Fabian. Now is the woodcock° near the gin°.

Affect me: like me   *Complexion:* personality.   *'Slight:* by G-d's light.
Employment: business.   *Woodcock:* stupid bird.   *Gin:* trap.

33

Toby. O, peace, and the spirit of humors intimate reading aloud to him.

Malvolio. By my life. This is my lady's hand. These be her very C's, her U's, and her T's; and thus makes she her great P's.

Andrew. Her C's, her U's, and her T's? Why that?

Malvolio. [Reading.] 'To the unknown beloved, this, and my good wishes.' Her very phrases! By your leave, wax. Soft°, and the impressure her Lucrece°, with which she uses to seal. 'Tis my lady. To whom should this be?
[Reading.] 'Jove knows I love,
         But who?
      Lips, do not move;
         No man must know.'
'No man must know.' What follows? The numbers altered!
'No man must know.'. . .If this should be thee, Malvolio?

Toby. Marry, hand thee, brock°!

Malvolio. [Reading.]
        'I may command thee where I adore,
           But silence, like a Lucrece knife,
        With bloodless stroke my heart doth gore,
           M.O.A.I. doth sway my life.'

Toby. Excellent wench°, say I!

Soft: wait a minute.   *Lucrece:* a virtuous and chaste Roman matron.   *Brock:* stinking fellow.   *Excellent wench:* clever girl.

Malvolio. 'M.O.A.I. doth sway my life.' Nay, but first, let
me see, let me see, let me see... 'I may command where
I adore.' Why she may command me: I serve her; she is
my lady...What should that alphabetical position
portend? If I could make that resemble something in me!
Softly, 'M.O.A.I.'...M—Malvolio. M.—Why that begins
my name.

Fabian. Did not I say he would work it out?

Malvolio. M, O, I, A. Every one of these letters are in my
name. Soft, here follows prose. *[Reading.]*

'In my stars I am above thee, but be not afraid of greatness. Some are born great, some achieve greatness and
some have greatness thrust upon them. Be opposite with
a kinsman, surly with servants. Remember who commended thy yellow stockings and wished to see thee ever
cross-gartered°. I say, remember. Farewell. She that would
alter services with thee,
                              'The Fortunate-Unhappy.'
I will be proud. I will baffle° Sir Toby, I will wash off
gross acquaintance. . . My lady loves me. She did com-
mend my yellow stockings of late, she did praise my leg
being crossgartered; and in this she manifests herself to
my love, and with a kind of injunction drives me to these
habits° of her liking. I thank my stars, I am happy. Jove
and my stars be praised. Here is yet a postscript. *[Reads.]*
'Thou canst not choose but know who I am. If thou
entertain'st my love, let it appear in thy smiling.
Therefore in my presence still smile, dear my sweet,
I prithee.' Jove, I thank thee. I will smile; I will do
everything that thou wilt have me. *[He exits.]*

Cross-gartered: garters crossed above and below the knee   *Baffle* disgrace.
Habits: dress.

Toby. I could marry this wench for this device.

Andrew. So could I too.

Maria. He will come to her in yellow stockings, and 'tis a color she abhors, and cross-gartered, a fashion she detests; and he will smile upon her, which will now be so unsuitable to her disposition, being addicted to a melancholy as she is, that it cannot but turn him into a notable contempt. If you will see it, follow me.

Toby. To the gates of Tartar°, thou most excellent devil of wit.

Andrew. I'll make one too.

They exit.

Tartar: Tartarus, section of hell reserved for the most evil.

ACT III, SCENE 1.
Olivia's Garden.

Enter Viola and Clown [with a tabor°].

Viola. Save thee, friend, and thy music. Dost thou live by thy tabor?

Clown. No, sir. I live by the church.

Viola. Art thou a churchman?

Clown. No such matter, sir. I do live by the church; for I do live at my house, and my house doth stand by the church.

Viola. I warrant thou art a merry fellow and carest for nothing.

Clown. Not so, sir; I do care for something; but in my conscience, sir, I do not care for you.

Viola. Art not thou the lady Olivia's fool?

Clown No, indeed, sir. The lady Olivia has no folly. She will keep no fools, sir, till she be married. I am indeed not her fool, but her corrupter of words.

Viola. I'll no more with thee. Hold, there's expenses for thee.

She gives him a coin.

Tabor: small drum.

39

Clown. Now Jove, in his next commodity of hair, send thee a beard.

Viola. By my troth, I'll tell thee, I am almost sick for one, though I would not have it grow on my chin. Is thy lady within?

Clown. My lady is within, sir. I will conster° to them whence you come. Who you are and what you would are out of my welkin°; I might say 'element,' but the word is over-worn.

He exits.

Viola. This fellow is wise enough to play the fool,
And to do that well craves a kind of wit.
He must observe their mood on whom he jests,
The quality of persons, and the time;
And like the haggard°, check at every feather
That comes before his eye. This is a practice
As full of labor as a wise man's art.

Enter Olivia and Maria.

Viola. Most excellent accomplished lady, the heavens rain odors on you. My matter hath no voice°, lady, but to your own most pregnant° and vouchsafed ear.

Olivia. Let the garden door be shut, and leave me to my hearing. *[Maria exits.]* Give me your hand, sir.

Viola. My duty, madam, and most humble service.

Conster: explain.   *Welkin:* sky.   *Haggard:* untrained hawk.   *Hath no voice:* can be told to no one.   *Pregnant:* receptive.

Olivia. What's your name?

Viola. Cesario is your servant's name, fair princess.

Olivia. My servant, sir? You are servant to the Count
   Orsino.

Viola. And he is yours, and his must needs be yours. Your
   servant's servant is your servant, madam. I come to whet
   your gentle thoughts on his behalf.

Olivia. O, by your leave, I pray you. I bade you never speak
   again on him.

Viola. Dear lady—

Olivia. Give me leave, beseech you…I did send,
   After the last enchantment you did here,
   A ring in chase of you. So did I abuse
   Myself, my servant, and, I fear me, you…
   So, let me hear you speak.

Viola.   I pity you.

Olivia. That's a degree° to love.

Viola. No not a grize; for 'tis a vulgar proof
   That very oft we pity enemies. *[She is about to leave.]*

Olivia. Stay.
   I prithee tell me what thou think'st of me.

Viola. That you do think you are not what you are.

Degree: step and grize [in the next line] is a synonym.

41

Olivia. If I think so, I think the same of you.

Viola. Then think you right. I am not what I am.

Olivia. I would you were as I would have you be.

Viola. Would it be better, madam, than I am?
I wish it might, for now I am your fool.

Olivia. Cesario, by the roses of the spring,
By maidhood, honor, truth, and everything,
I love thee so that, maugre° all thy pride,
Nor wit, nor reason can my passion hide.

Viola. By innocence I swear, and by my youth,
I have one heart, one bosom, and one truth,
And that no woman has; nor ever none
Shall mistress be of it, save I alone.
And so adieu, good madam. Never more
Will I my master's tears to you deplore.

She begins to leave.

Olivia. Yet come again; for thou perhaps mayst move
That heart which now abhors to like his love.

Viola leaves and Olivia exits in the same direction.

Maugre: despite.

ACT III, SCENE 2.
OLIVIA'S HOUSE.

Enter Sir Toby, Sir Andrew, and Fabian.

Andrew. No, faith, I'll not stay a jot longer.

Toby. The reason, dear venom°; give thy reason.

Andrew. Marry, I saw your niece do more favors to the Count's servingman than ever she bestowed upon me. I saw't in th' orchard.

Fabian. She did show favor to the youth in your sight only to exasperate you, to awake your dormouse valor, to put fire in your heart and brimstone in your liver. You should then have accosted her, and with some excellent jests, fire-new from mint, you should have banged the youth into dumbness.

Toby. Build me thy fortunes upon the basis of valor. Challenge me the Count's youth to fight with him; hurt him in eleven places. My niece shall take note of it, and assure thyself there is no love-broker in the world can more prevail in man's commendation with woman than report of valor.

Fabian. There is no way but this, Sir Andrew.

Andrew. Will either of you bear me a challenge to him?

Venom: [Sir Andrew is filled with anger.]

43

Toby. Go, write it in a martial hand. Be curst and brief; it is
   no matter how witty, so it be eloquent and full of inven-
   tion. Let there be gall° enough in thy ink, though thou
   write with a goose-pen, no matter. About it!

Andrew. Where shall I find you?

Toby. We'll call thee° at the cubiculo°. Go!

Exit Sir Andrew.

Fabian. This is a dear manikin° to you, Sir Toby.

Toby. I have been dear to him, lad, some two thousand
   strong or so.

Fabian. We shall have a rare letter from him.

Enter Maria.

Toby. Look where the youngest wren of mine comes.

Maria. He does obey every point of the letter that I
   dropped to betray him. You have not seen such a thing as
   'tis. I know my lady will strike him. If she do, he'll smile,
   and take't for a great favor.

Toby. Come bring us, bring us where he is.

They exit.

Gall: (1) ingredient of ink; (2) rancor.   *Call thee:* call for you.   *Cubiculo:* little
chamber.   *Manikin:* puppet.

ACT III, SCENE 3.
A STREET IN ILLYRIA.

Enter Sebastian and Antonio.

Antonio. I could not stay behind you.
  Your being skilless° in these parts; which to a stranger,
  Unguided and unfriended, often prove
  Rough and unhospitable.

Sebastian.   My kind Antonio,
  I can no other answer make but thanks. What's to do?
  Shall we go see the relics° of the town?

Antonio. Would you'd pardon me.
  I do not without danger walk these streets.
  Once in a sea-fight 'gainst the Count his galleys
  I did some service; of such note indeed
  That, were I ta'en here, it would scarce be answered°.

Sebastian. Belike you slew great numbers of his people?

Antonio. Th' offense is not of such a bloody nature.
  It might have since been answered in repaying
  What we took from them, which for traffic's° sake
  Most of our city did. Only myself stood out;
  For which, if I be lapsed° in this place,
  I shall pay dear.

Sebastian. Do not then walk too open.

Antonio. It doth not fit me. Hold, sir, here's my purse. In
  the south suburbs at the Elephant° is best to lodge. There
  shall you have me.

Skilless. without knowledge.   *Relics.* monuments.   *Answered:* atoned for.
Traffic's: trade's.   *Lapsed·* taken by surprise.   *Elephant:* an inn.

Sebastian. Why I your purse?

Antonio. Haply your eye shall light upon some toy°
   You have desire to purchase, and your store°
   I think is not for idle markets°, sir.

Sebastian. I'll be your purse-bearer, and leave you for
   An hour.

Antonio. To th' Elephant.

Sebastian.   I do remember.

They exit.

Toy: trifle.   *Store:* money.   *Idle markets:* useless trinkets.

ACT III, SCENE 4.
OLIVIA'S GARDEN

Enter Olivia and Maria.

Olivia. Where is Malvolio?
  I have sent after him; he says he'll come.

Maria. He's coming, madam, but in a very strange manner.
  He does nothing but smile.

Enter Malvolio.

Olivia. How now, Malvolio?

Malvolio. Sweet lady, ho, ho!

Olivia. Smil'st thou? I sent for thee upon a sad occasion.

Malvolio. Sad, lady? I could be sad. This does make some
  obstruction in the blood, this cross-gartering; but what of
  that?

Olivia. Why, how dost thou, man? What is the matter with
  thee?

Malvolio. Not black in my mind, though yellow in my
  legs...I think we know the sweet Roman hand.

Olivia. Wilt thou go to bed, Malvolio?

Malvolio. To bed? Aye, sweetheart, and I'll come to thee.

Olivia. G-d comfort thee. Why dost thou smile so, and kiss thy hand so oft?

Maria. Why appear you with this ridiculous boldness before my lady?

Malvolio. 'Be not afraid of greatness.' 'Tis well writ.

Olivia. What mean'st thou by that, Malvolio?

Malvolio. 'Some are born great.'

Olivia. Ha?

Malvolio. 'And some have greatness thrust upon them.'

Olivia. Heaven restore thee!

Malvolio. 'Remember who commended thy yellow stockings.'

Olivia. The yellow stockings?

Malvolio. 'And wished to see the cross-gartered.'

Olivia. Cross-gartered? Why this is very midsummer madness.

Enter Fabian.

Fabian. Madam, the young gentleman of the Count Orsino's is returned. I could hardly entreat him back.

Olivia. I'll come to him. *[Fabian exits.]* Good Maria, let
this fellow be looked to. Let some of my people have a
special care of him. I would not have him miscarry° for
the half of my dowry.

Olivia and Maria exit.

Malvolio. Nothing that can be can come between me and
the full prospect of my hopes. Well, Jove, not I, is the
doer of this, and he is to be thanked.

*Exit Malvolio as Sir Toby, Sir Andrew, and Fabian enter from
a different direction.*

Andrew. Here's the challenge; read it. I warrant there's
vinegar and pepper in't.

Fabian. Is't so saucy?

Andrew. Aye, is't, I warrant him. Do but read.

Toby. Give me. *[Reads.]* 'Youth, whatsoever thou art, thou
art but a scurvy fellow.'

Fabian. Good, and valiant.

Toby. 'Thou com'st to the lady Olivia, and in my sight she
uses thee kindly. But thou liest in thy throat; that is not
the matter I challenge thee for.'

Miscarry: come to harm.

Fabian. Very brief, and to exceeding good sense-less.

Enter Maria. Fabian encourages her to listen.

Toby. [Reads.] 'I will waylay thee going home; where if it be thy chance to kill me. . .'

Fabian. Good!

Toby. 'Thou kill'st me like a rogue and villain. Fare thee well, and G-d have mercy upon one of our souls. He may have mercy upon mine, but my hope is better, and so look to thyself. Thy friend, as thou usest him, and thy sworn enemy,
                    Andrew Aguecheek,'
If this letter move him not, his legs cannot. I'll give't to him.

Maria. You may have very fit occasion for't. He is now in some commerce with my lady and will by and by depart.

Toby. Go, Sir Andrew. Scout me for him at the comer of the orchard. So soon as ever thou seest him, draw; and as thou draw'st, swear horrible; for it comes to pass oft that a terrible oath, with a swaggering accent sharply twanged off, gives manhood more approbation° than ever proof itself would have earned him. Away!

Andrew. Nay, let me alone for swearing.

Andrew exits.

Gives manhood more approbation: a great reputation for courage.

Toby. Now will not I deliver this letter. I will deliver his
   challenge by word of mouth, set upon Aguecheek a
   notable report of valor, and drive the gentleman into
   a most hideous opinion of his rage, skill, fury, and
   impetuosity. This will so fright them both that they will
   kill one another by the look, like cockatrices°.

Enter Olivia and Viola.

Fabian. Here he comes with your niece. Give them way till
   he take leave, and presently after him.

Toby. I will meditate the while on some horrid message for
   a challenge.

Exit Sir Toby, Fabian, and Maria.

Olivia. Here, wear this jewel for me; 'tis my picture.
   Refuse it not; it hath no tongue to vex you.
   And I beseech you, come again tomorrow.
   What shall you ask of me that I'll deny,
   That honor, saved, may upon asking give?

Viola. Nothing but this; your true love for my master.

Olivia. How with mine honor may I give him that
   Which I have given to you?

Viola.   I will acquit you.

Cockatrices: serpents supposedly able to kill with a glance.

51

Olivia. Well, come again tomorrow. Fare thee well.
  A fiend like thee might bear my soul to hell.

Viola exits as Sir Toby and Maria enter.

Toby. Gentleman, G-d save thee.

Viola. And you, sir.

Toby.   Of what nature the wrongs are thou hast done
  him, I know not; but thy interceptor, full of despite,
  attends thee at the orchard end. Dismount thy tuck°,
  for thy assailant is quick, skillful and deadly.

Viola. You mistake, sir. I am sure no man hath any quarrel
  to me. My remembrance is very free and clear from any
  image of offense done to any man.

Toby. You'll find it otherwise, I assure you.

Viola. I pray you, sir, what is he?

Toby. He is a devil in private brawl. Souls and bodies hath
  he divorced three.

Viola. I am no fighter. I beseech you do me this courteous
  office, as to know of the knight what my offense to him
  is. It is something of my negligence, nothing of my
  purpose.

Toby. I will do so. Signoir Fabian, stay you by this
  gentleman till my return. *[He exits.]*

Dismount thy tuck: Draw your rapier.

Viola. Pray you, sir, do you know of this matter?

Fabian. I know the knight is incensed against you, even to a mortal arbitrement°; but nothing of the circumstance more.

Viola. I beseech you. What matter of man is he?

Fabian. He is indeed, sir, the most skillful, bloody and fatal opposite that you could possibly have found in any part of Illyria…I will make your peace with him if I can.

Viola. I shall be much bound to you for't. I am one that had rather go with sir priest than sir knight. I care not who knows so much of my mettle.

They exit as Sir Toby and Sir Andrew enter.

Toby. Why, man, he's a very devil; I have not seen such a firago°. I had a pass with him, rapier, scabbard, and all, and he gives me the stuck-in° with such a mortal motion that it is inevitable.

Andrew. Pox on't, I'll not meddle with him.

Toby. Stand here; make a good show on't. This shall end without the perdition of souls°. Draw for the supportance of his vow. He protests he will not hurt you.

Viola. [Aside.] Pray G-d defend me! A little thing would make me tell them how much I lack of a man.

Mortal arbitrement: dueling to the death.   *Firago:* one who acts like a man. (The joke, of course, is on Sir Toby.)   *Stuck-in:* thrust.   *Perdition of souls:* loss of lives.

Fabian. Give ground if you see him furious.

Toby. Come, Sir Andrew, there's no remedy. The gentleman will for his honor's sake have one bout with you. He has promised me, as he is a gentleman and a soldier, he will not hurt you. Come on, to't.

Andrew. Pray G-d he keep his oath!

He draws his sword as Antonio enters.

Viola. I assure you 'tis against my will.

She draws.

Antonio. Put up your sword. If this young gentleman
Have done offenses, I take the fault on me.

Toby. You, sir? Why, what are you?

Antonio. [Draws.] One, sir, that for his love dares yet do more than you have heard him brag to you he will.

Toby. Nay, if you be an undertaker, I am for you.

He draws as officers enter.

Fabian. O good Sir Toby, hold. Here come the officers.

Toby. [To Antonio.] I'll be with you anon°.

Anon: soon.

Viola. [To Sir Andrew.] Pray, sir, put your sword up, if you
   please.

Andrew. Marry, will I, sir; and for that I promised you, I'll
   be as good as my word. He will bear you easily, and reins
   well.

Officer 1. This is the man; do thy office.

Officer 2. Antonio, I arrest thee at the suit of Count
   Orsino.

Antonio. You do mistake me, sir.

Officer 1. No, sir, no jot. I know your favor well,
   Though now you have no sea-cap on your head.
   Take him away. He knows I know him well.

Antonio. I obey. *[To Viola.]* I must entreat you some of that
   money.

Viola. What money, sir?
   For that fair kindness you have showed me here,
   I'll lend you something. My having is not much.
   Hold, there's half my coffer°.

Antonio.   Will you deny me now?
   Is't possible that my deserts to you
   Can lack persuasion? Do not tempt my misery,
   Lest that it make me unsound a man
   As to upbraid you with those kindnesses
   That I have done for you.

Coffer: strong box or store of wealth.

Viola.   I know of none,
  Nor know I you by voice or any feature.

Antonio. O heavens themselves!

Officer 2.   Come, sir, I pray you go.

Antonio. Let me speak a little. This youth that you see here
  I snatched one half out of the jaws of death;
  Relieved him with such sanctity of love,
  And to his image, which methought did promise
  Most venerable worth, did I devotion.

Officer 2. What's that to us? The time goes by. Away.

Antonio. But, O, how vile an idol proves this god!
  Thou hast, Sebastian, done good feature shame.

Officer 1. The man grows mad; away with him! Come,
  come, sir.

Antonio. Lead on.

Officers exit with Antonio.

Viola. Methinks his words do from such passion fly
  That he believes himself; so do not I.
  He named Sebastian. I my brother know
  Yet living in my glass°. Even such and so
  In favor was my brother, and he went
  Still in this fashion, color, ornament,

Yet living in my glass: i.e. whenever I look in a mirror.

56

[Viola.] For him I imitate. O, if it prove,
   Tempests are kind, and salt waves fresh in love!

She exits.

Toby. A very dishonest paltry boy, and more a coward
   than a hare. His dishonesty appears in leaving his friend
   here in necessity and denying him.

Fabian. A coward, a most devout coward.

Andrew. 'Slid, I'll after him again and beat him.

Toby. Do. Cuff him soundly, but never draw thy sword.

Andrew. An I do not! *[Sir Andrew exits.]*

Fabian. Come, let's see the event.

Toby. I dare lay any money 'twill be nothing yet.

They exit.

ACT IV, SCENE 1
BEFORE OLIVIA'S HOUSE.

Enter Sebastian and Clown.

Clown. Will you make me believe that I am not sent for
you?

Sebastian. Go to, go to, thou art a foolish fellow. Let me be
clear of thee.

Clown. Well held out°, in faith! No, I do not know you;
nor am I not sent to you by my lady, to bid you come
speak with her; nor your name is not Cesario; nor this is
not my nose neither. Nothing that is so is so.

Sebastian. I prithee, depart from me. There's money for
thee. If you tarry longer, I shall give worse payment.

Enter Sir Toby, Sir Andrew, and Fabian.

Andrew. Now, sir, have I met you again? There's for thee.

Andrew strikes Sebastian.

Sebastian. [Striking Sir Andrew.] Why, there's for thee, and
there, and there! Are all the people mad?

Toby. Hold, sir! *[Seizes Sebastian.]*

Clown. This will I tell my lady straight. I would not be in
some of your coats for two-pence.

Clown exits.

Held out: kept up.

60

Toby. Come on, sir; hold!

Andrew. I'll have an action of battery against him°, if there
be any law in Illyria. Though I struck him first, yet it's no
matter for that.

Sebastian. Let go thy hand!

Toby. Come, sir, I will not let you go.

Sebastian. I will be free from thee. *[Frees himself.]*
What wouldst thou now? If thou darest tempt me
further, draw thy sword.

Sebastian draws his sword.

Toby. What, what? Nay then, I must have an ounce or two
of this malapert° blood from you.

Sir Toby draws his sword as Olivia enters.

Olivia. Hold, Toby! On thy life I charge thee hold!

Toby. Madam.

Olivia. Out of my sight! Rudesby°, be gone.

Sir Toby, Sir Andrew, and Fabian exit.

I'll have...against him: I'll have him charged with assault and battery.   *Malapert:*
impudent.   *Rudesby:* unmannerly fellow.

Olivia.   Be not offended, dear Cesario.
I prithee, gentle friend, go with me to my house,
And hear thou there how many fruitless pranks
This ruffian hath botched up°, that thou thereby
Mayst smile at this.

Sebastian. What relish is in this? How runs the stream?
Or I am mad, or else this is a dream.
If it be thus to dream, still let me sleep!

Olivia
~~Viola.~~ Nay, come, I prithee. Would thou'dst be ruled by me!

Sebastian. Madam, I will.

Olivia
~~Viola.~~ O, say so, and so be.

They exit.

ACT IV, SCENE 2.
WITHIN OLIVIA'S HOUSE.

*Sir Toby and Clown enter. Malvolio is confined to a part of
the room that resembles a dark, damp basement cellar.*

Toby. Nay, put on this gown and this beard; make him
believe thou art Sir Topas ° the curate; do it quickly!

Clown. Well, I'll put it on, and I will dissemble° myself in't,
and I would I were the first that ever dissembled in such
a gown. I am not tall enough to become the function°.

Toby. [Loudly but not seen.] Jove bless thee, Master Parson.

Botched up: contrived.   *Topas:* a gem that supposedly cured insanity.   *Dissemble*
disguise.   *Function:* the function of a clergyman.

Clown. [Loudly, in a disguised voice.] Bonos dies°, Sir Toby.

Toby. [Softly.] To him, Sir Topas.

Sir Toby exits.

Clown. What ho, I say. Peace in this prison!

Malvolio. Who calls?

Clown. Sir Topas, the curate, who comes to visit Malvolio the lunatic.

Malvolio. Sir Topas, good Sir Topas, go to my lady.

Clown. Out, hyperbolic fiend°! How vexest thou this man! Talkest thou nothing but of ladies.

Malvolio. Sir Topas, never was man thus wronged. Good Sir Topas, do not think I am mad. They have laid me here in hideous darkness.

Clown. Fie, thou dishonest Satan. Say'st thou that house is dark?

Malvolio. As hell, Sir Topas.

Clown. Madman, thou errest. I say there is no darkness but ignorance.

Bonos dies: good day.   *Hyperbolic fiend:* i.e. monstrous devil that has taken over Malvolio.

Malvolio. I say this house is as dark as ignorance, though ignorance were as dark as hell. I am no more mad than you.

Clown. Fare thee well. Remain thou still in darkness. Fare thee well. *[Quickly moves just out of Malvolio's sight to remove his disguise.]*

Malvolio. Sir Topas, Sir Topas!

Clown. [Singing.] 'Hey, Robin, jolly Robin,
            Tell me how thy lady does.'

Malvolio. Fool.

Clown. Who calls, ha?

Malvolio. Good fool, as ever thou wilt deserve well at my hand, help me to a candle, and pen, ink, and paper. As I am a gentleman, I will live to be thankful to thee for't.

Clown. Master Malvolio?

Malvolio. Aye, good fool.

Clown. Alas, sir, how fell you besides your five wits?

Malvolio. They have here propertied° me; keep me in darkness, end ministers to me, asses, and do all they can to face me out of my wits.

Propertied: locked me up like a piece of furniture.

Clown. Advise you what you say. The minister is here.
   [Moves out of Malvolio's sight.] Malvolio, Malvolio, thy
   wits the heavens restore. Endeavor thyself to sleep and
   leave thy vain bibble babble°.

Malvolio. Sir Topas.

Clown. *[Disguised voice.]* Maintain no words with him,
   good fellow. *[Own voice.]* Who, I sir? Not I, sir. G-d b'
   wi' you, good Sir Topas. *[Disguised voice.]* Marry, amen.
   [Own voice.] I will sir, I will.

Malvolio. Fool, fool, fool, I say!

Clown. *[Returning to Malvolio.]* Alas, sir, be patient. What
   say you, sir? I am shent° for speaking to you.

Malvolio. I am as well in my wits as any man in Illyria.

Clown. Well-a-day° that you were sir.

Malvolio. Good fool, some ink, paper, and light; and con-
   vey what I will set down to my lady. It shall advantage
   thee more than ever the bearing of letter did.

Clown. I will help you to't.

They exit.

Bibble babble· ranting and raving   *Shent:* rebuked.

ACT IV, SCENE 3.
OLIVIA'S HOUSE.

Enter Sebastian.

Sebastian. This is the air; that is the glorious sun;
    This pearl she gave me, I do feel't and see't;
    And though 'tis wonder that enwraps me thus,
    Yet 'tis not madness. Where's Antonio then?
    I could not find him at the Elephant;
    Yet there he was°, and there I found this credit°,
    That he did range the town to seek me out.
    His counsel now might do me golden service.

Enter Olivia and Priest.

Olivia. Now go with me and with this holy man
    Into the chantry° by. There, before him,
    And underneath that consecrated roof,
    Plight me the full assurance of your faith,
    That my most jealous° and too doubtful soul
    may live at peace. He shall conceal it
    While you are willing it shall come to note,
    What time we will our celebration keep
    According to my birth. What do you say?

Sebastian. I'll follow this good man and go with you
    And having sworn truth, ever will be true.

Olivia. Then lead the way, good father, and heavens so shine
    That they may fairly note this act of mine. *[They exit.]*

Well-a-day: alas. *Was:* had been. *Credit:* information. *Chantry:* chapel.
Jealous: anxious.

Actor / Director Notes

ACT V, SCENE 1.
Before Olivia's house.

Enter Clown and Fabian.

Fabian. Now as thou lov'st me, let me see his letter.

Clown. Good Master Fabian, grant me another request.

Fabian. Anything.

Clown. Do not desire to see this letter.

Enter Duke, Viola, Curio, and Lords.

Duke. How dost thou, my good fellow?

Clown. Truly, sir, the better for my foes, and the worse for my friends.

Duke. Just the contrary: the better for thy friends.

Clown. No, sir, the worse.

Duke. How can that be?

Clown. Marry, sir, they praise me and make an ass of me. Now my foes tell me plainly I am an ass; so that by my foes, sir, I profit in the knowledge of myself, and by my friends I am abused.

Duke. Why this is excellent. There's gold for you.
   If you will let your lady know I am here to speak with
   her, and bring her along with you, it may awake my
   bounty further.

Clown. Marry, sir, lullaby to your bounty till I come again.
   I go sir.

Clown exits as Antonio and the two officers enter.

Viola. Here comes the man, sir, that did rescue me.

Duke. That face of his I do remember well;
   Yet when I saw it last, it was besmeared
   As black as Vulcan° in the smoke of war.

Officer 1. Orsino, this is that Antonio
   That took the *Phoenix* and her fraught° from Candy°;
   And this is he that did the *Tiger* board
   When your young nephew Titus lost his leg.

Viola. He did me kindness, sir; drew on my side;
   But in conclusion put strange speech upon me.

Duke. Notable pirate, thou salt-water thief,
   What foolish boldness brought thee to their mercies
   Whom thou in terms so bloody and so dear
   Hast made thine enemies?

Vulcan: patron of metal workers, blackened by the smoky fire of his smithy.
Fraught: cargo.   *Candy:* Crete.

Antonio. Orsino, noble sir, Antonio never yet was thief or
  pirate, though I confess, on base and ground enough,
  Orsino's enemy. A witchcraft drew me hither. That most
  ungrateful boy there by your side from the rude sea's
  enraged and foamy mouth did I redeem. For his sake did
  I expose myself into the danger of this adverse town;
  drew to defend him when he was beset; where being
  apprehended, denied me my own purse, which I had
  recommended° to his use not half an hour before.

Viola.   How can this be?

Duke. When came he to this town?

Antonio. Today, my lord; and for three months before,
  No int'rim, not a minute's vacancy,
  Both day and night did we keep company.

Enter Olivia and Attendants.

Duke. Here comes the Countess; now heaven walks on
  earth. But for thee, fellow—fellow, thy words are madness. Three months this youth hath tended upon me;
  But more of that anon. Take him aside.

Officers move out of the way with Antonio.

Olivia. Cesario, you do not keep promise with me.

Recommended: entrusted.

71

Viola. Madam?

Duke. Gracious Olivia—

Olivia. What do you say, Cesario? *[To the Duke.]* Good my
lord.

Viola. My lord would speak; my duty hushes me.

Olivia. If it be aught to the old tune, my lord,
It is as fat and fulsome° to mine ear
As howling after music.

Duke.   Still so cruel?

Olivia. Still so constant, lord.

Duke.   You uncivil lady,
To whose ingrate and unauspicious altars
My soul the faithful'st off'rings have breathed out
That e'er devotion tendered. What shall I do?

Olivia. Even what it please my lord, that shall become him.

Duke. This your minion, whom I know you love,
And whom, by heaven I swear, I tender dearly,
Him will I tear out of that cruel eye
Where he sits crowned in his master's spite°.

Duke. Come, boy, with me. My thoughts are ripe in
mischief. I'll sacrifice the lamb that I do love
To spite a raven's heart within a dove.

Fulsome: offensive.   *In...spite:* despite his master.

72

Viola. And I, most jocund, apt, and willingly,
    To do you rest a thousand deaths would die.

The Duke starts to exit and Viola follows.

Olivia. Where goes Cesario?

Viola.   After him I love
    More than I love these eyes, more than my life,
    More, by all mores°, than ever I shall love wife.

Olivia. Aye me detested! How am I beguiled!

Viola. Who does beguile you? Who does do you wrong?

Olivia. Hast thou forgot thyself? Is it so long?
    Call forth the holy father. *[Exit an Attendant.]*

Duke. [To Viola.]   Come, away!

Olivia. Whither, my lord? Cesario, husband, stay.

Duke. Husband?

Olivia.   Aye, husband. Can he that deny?

Duke. Her husband, sirrah?

Viola.   No, my lord, not I.

Mores: equal comparisons.

73

Olivia. Alas, it is the baseness of thy fear
   That makes thee strangle thy propriety°.
   Fear not, Cesario; take thy fortunes up;
   Be that thou know'st thou art, and then thou art
   As great as that thou fear'st.

Enter Priest.

Olivia.   O, welcome, father!
   Father, I charge thee by thy reverence
   Here to unfold what thou dost know
   Hath newly passed between this youth and me.

Priest. A contract of eternal bond of love,
   Confirmed my mutual joinder of your hands,
   Attested by the holy close of lips,
   Strength'ned by interchangement of your rings;
   And all the ceremony of this compact
   Sealed in my function, by my testimony.

Duke. O thou dissembling cub, what wilt thou be
   When time hath sowed a grizzle on thy case°?
   Farewell, and take her; but direct thy feet
   Where thou and I, henceforth, may never meet.

Enter Sir Andrew.

Andrew. For the love of G-d, a surgeon! Send one presently
   to Sir Toby.

Olivia. What's the matter?

Andrew. He has broke my head across, and has given Sir
   Toby a bloody coxcomb° too.

Propriety: identity.   *Grizzle on thy case:* gray hair on thy skin.   *Coxcomb:* head.

Olivia. Who has done this, Sir Andrew?

Andrew. The Count's gentleman, one Cesario. We took him
for a coward, but he's the very devil incardinate°.

Viola. Why do you speak to me? I never hurt you. You
drew your sword upon me without cause, but I bespake
you fair and hurt you not.

Enter Sir Toby and Clown.

Andrew. Here comes Sir Toby halting°; you shall hear more.

Duke. How now, gentleman? How is't with you?

Toby. That's all one! Has hurt me, and there's th' end on't.
Sot, didst see Dick Surgeon, sot?

Clown. O, he's drunk.

Olivia. Away with him!

Andrew. I'll help you, Sir Toby, because we'll be dressed°
together.

Sir Toby. Will you help? An asshead and a coxcomb and a
knave, a thin-faced knave, a gull?

Olivia. Get him to bed, and let his hurt be looked to.

Exit Clown, Fabian, Toby, and Andrew as Sebastian enters.

Sebastian. I am sorry, madam, I have hurt your kinsman.

Incardinate: incarnate.   *Halting.* limping.   *Dressed:* bandaged.

All freeze, looking at Sebastian and Viola.

[Sebastian.] You throw a strange regard upon me.

Duke. One face, one voice, one habit°, and two persons...
    A natural perspective that is and is not.

Sebastian. Antonio, O my dear Antonio, How have the
    hours racked and tortured me since I have lost thee!

Antonio. Sebastian are you?

Sebastian.   Fear'st thou that, Antonio?

Antonio. How have you made division of yourself?

Olivia. Most wonderful.

Sebastian. Do I stand there? I never had a brother;
    I had a sister,
    Whom the blind waves and surges have devoured.
    Of charity, what kin are you to me?
    What countryman? What name? What parentage?

Viola. Of Messaline; Sebastian was my father;
    Such a Sebastian was my brother too;
    So went he suited to his watery tomb.

Sebastian. Were you a woman, as the rest goes even,
    I should my tears let fall upon your cheek
    And say, 'Thrice welcome, drowned Viola!'

Habit: dress.

76

Viola. My father died when Viola from her birth
  Had numb'red thirteen years.

Sebastian. O, that record is lively in my soul!
  He finished indeed his mortal act
  That day that made my sister thirteen years.

Viola. If nothing lets to make us happy both
  but this my masculine usurped attire,
  Do not embrace me till each circumstance
  Of place, time, fortune do cohere and jump
  That I am Viola.

Sebastian. [*To Olivia.*] So comes it, lady, you have been
  mistook.
  But nature to her bias drew in that.
  You would have been contracted to a maid;
  Nor are you therein, by my life, deceived,
  You are betrothed both to a maid and man.

Duke. [*To Viola.*] Boy, thou hast said to me a thousand
  times thou never shouldst love woman like to me.

Viola. All those sayings will I overswear.

Duke.   Give me thy hand,
  And let me see thee in thy woman's weeds°.

Viola. The captain that did bring me first on shore
  Hath my maid's garments. He upon some action°
  Is now in durance, at Malvolio's suit,
  A gentleman, and follower of my lady's.

Olivia. And yet alas, now I remember me,
  They say, poor gentleman, he's much distract.

Weeds: garments.   *Action:* legal obligation.

Enter Clown with a letter, and Fabian.

Olivia. How does Malvolio, sirrah?

Clown. Truly, madam, he holds Beelzebub at the stave's
end° as well as a man in his case may do. Has here writ a
letter to you and says you wronged him. *[Hands letter to
Olivia.]*

Olivia. Did he write this?

Clown. Aye, madam.

Olivia. See him delivered, Fabian; bring him hither.

Fabian exits.

Olivia. My lord, so please you, these things further thought
  On, to think me as well a sister as a wife,
  One day shall crown the alliance on't, so please you,
  Here at my house and at my proper cost.

Duke. Madam, I am most apt t' embrace your offer.
  [To Viola.] Your master quits you; and for your service
    done on him,   Gender
  So much against the mettle of your ~~sex,~~
  So far beneath your soft and tender breeding,
  And since you called me master for so long,
  Here is my hand; you shall from this time be
  Your master's mistress.

Olivia. A sister! You are she. *[Enter Fabian and Malvolio.]*

Duke. Is this the madman?

Holds...end: holds the devil off.

78

Olivia. Aye, my lord, this same. How now, Malvolio?

Malvolio. Madam, you have done me wrong,
   Notorious wrong.

Olivia.   Have I, Malvolio? No.

Malvolio. Lady, you have. Pray you peruse that letter.
   You must not now deny it is your hand.
   Tell me, in the modesty of honor,
   Why you have given me such clear lights of favor,
   Bade me come smiling and cross-gartered to you,
   And to put on yellow stockings?

Olivia. Alas, Malvolio, this is not my writing, 'tis Maria's
   hand. And now I do bethink me, it was she
   First told me thou wast mad. Thou camest in smiling,
   And in such forms which here were presupposed
   Upon thee in the letter.

Fabian.   Good madam, hear me speak,
   And let no quarrel, nor no brawl to come,
   Taint the condition of this present hour.
   Most freely I confess myself and Toby
   Set this device against Malvolio here,
   Upon some stubborn and uncourteous parts
   We had conceived against him. Maria writ
   The letter, at Sir Toby's great importance,
   In recompense whereof he hath married her.

Olivia. Alas, poor fool, how have they baffled thee!

Clown. I was one sir, in this interlude, one Sir Topas, sir;

[Voice of Topas.] 'By the Lord, fool, I am not mad.'

Malvolio. I'll be revenged on the whole pack of you.

Malvolio exits.

Olivia. He hath been notoriously abused.

Duke. Pursue him and entreat him to a peace.
  He hath not told us of the captain yet.
  Meantime, sweet sister,
  We will not part from hence. Cesario, come.
  But when in other habits you are seen,
  Orsino's mistress and his fancy's queen.

Exit all but Clown.

Clown. [Sings.]
        When that I was a little tiny boy,
            With a hey, ho, the wind and the rain,
        A foolish thing was but a toy,
            For the rain it raineth every day.

        But when I came, alas, to wive,
            With hey, ho, the wind and the rain,
        By swaggering could I never thrive,
            For the rain it raineth every day.

        A great while ago the world begun,
            With hey, ho the wind and the rain;
        But that's all one, our play is done,
            And we'll strive to please you every day.

He exits.

The end.

Other Fine Titles From
Five Star Publications, Incorporated

Shakespeare: To Teach or Not to Teach

By Cass Foster and Lynn G. Johnson
The answer is a resounding "To Teach!" There's nothing dull about this guide for anyone teaching Shakespeare in the classroom, with activities such as crossword puzzles, a scavenger hunt, warm-up games, and costume and scenery suggestions. ISBN 1-877749-03-6

The Sixty-Minute Shakespeare Series

By Cass Foster
Not enough time to tackle the unabridged versions of the world's most widely read playwright? Pick up a copy of *Romeo and Juliet* (ISBN 1-877749-38-9), *A Midsummer Night's Dream* (ISBN 1-877749-37-0), *Hamlet* (ISBN 1-877749-40-0), *Macbeth* (ISBN 1-877749-41-9), *Much Ado About Nothing* (ISBN 1-877749-42-7), and *Twelfth Night* (ISBN 1-877749-39-7) and discover how much more accessible Shakespeare can be to you and your students.

Shakespeare for Children: The Story of Romeo and Juliet

By Cass Foster
Adults shouldn't keep a classic this good to themselves. This fully illustrated book makes the play easily understandable to young readers, yet it is faithful to the spirit of the original. A *Benjamin Franklin Children's Storybooks Award* nominee. ISBN 0-9619853-3-x

The Adventures of Andi O'Malley

By Celeste Messer

(1) Angel Experiment JR134
Ashley Layne is the richest and most popular girl in school. In an unusual twist, Andi is given the opportunity to know what it's truly like to be Ashley Layne. Travel with Andi as she discovers that things are not always as they seem. ISBN 0-9702171-0-2

(2) The Broken Wing
Andi is visited by a little angel who needs her help in more ways than one. The angel has broken her wing in a midair collision with another, larger angel and desperately needs Andi to hide her while she heals. Rather than hide her, Andi takes the little angel to school with her where no one could have expected the lessons they would learn! ISBN 0-9702171-1-0

(3) The Gift
Andi receives an assignment from her guardian angel. At first, she's excited, but she becomes furious when she realizes what the job involves. Although Andi tries desperately to get out of completing her assignment, she learns there is no turning back. What happens in the end could only happen to Andi O'Malley! ISBN 0-9702171-3-7

Other Fine Titles From
Five Star Publications, Incorporated

Most titles are available through
www.BarnesandNoble.com and www.amazon.com

(4) Circle of Light

The world is about to be taken over by Zykien, the most evil of all angels of darkness. With the help of the rather odd-looking Miss Bluebonnet, Andi and her friends discover the incredible power of goodness that can result when people work together. Even the Tashonians, the tiniest of creatures, play an important role in restoring peace and love to the world.
ISBN 0-9702171-2-9

(5) Three Miracles

Three young people are in a terrible accident caused by a drunk driver. Their voices are heard— but only by Andi's friend Troy. When he proves to Andi and her sister and brother that he's not making it up, the three voices give them three tasks that will change their lives and the lives of several others forever.
ISBN 0-9702171-4-5

Letters of Love: Stories from the Heart
Edited by Salvatore Caputo
In this warm collection of love letters and stories, a group of everyday people share hopes, dreams, and experiences of love: love won, love lost, and love found again. Most of all, they share their belief that love is a blessing that makes life's challenges worthwhile.   ISBN 1-877749-35-4

Linda F. Radke's Promote Like a Pro: Small Budget, Big Show
By Linda F. Radke
In this step-by-step guide, self-publishers can learn how to use the print and broadcast media, public relations, the Internet, public speaking, and other tools to market books—without breaking the bank! In *Linda F. Radke's Promote Like a Pro: Small Budget, Big Show*, a successful publisher and a group of insiders offer self-publishers valuable information about promoting books.
ISBN 1-877749-36-2

The Economical Guide to Self-Publishing: How to Produce and Market Your Book on a Budget
By Linda F. Radke
This book is a must-have for anyone who is or wants to be a self-publisher. It is a valuable step-by-step guide for producing and promoting your book effectively, even on a limited budget. The book is filled with tips on avoiding common, costly mistakes and provides resources that can save you lots of money—not to mention headaches. A *Writer's Digest Book Club* selection.   ISBN 1-877749-16-8

That Hungarian's in My Kitchen
By Linda F. Radke
You won't want that Hungarian to leave your kitchen after you've tried some of the 125 Hungarian-American Kosher recipes that fill this delightful cookbook. Written for both the novice cook and the sophisticated chef, the cookbook comes complete with "Aunt Ethel's Helpful Hints."   ISBN 1-877749-28-1

Other Fine Titles From
Five Star Publications, Incorporated

Most titles are available through
www.BarnesandNoble.com and www.amazon.com

Kosher Kettle: International Adventures in Jewish Cooking

By Sybil Ruth Kaplan, Foreword by Joan Nathan

With more than 350 recipes from 27 countries, this is one Kosher cookbook you don't want to be without. It includes everything from wheat halva from India to borrekas from Greece. Five Star Publications is donating a portion of all sales of *Kosher Kettle* to MAZON: A Jewish Response to Hunger. A *Jewish Book Club* selection. ISBN 1-877749-19-2

Passover Cookery

By Joan Kekst

Whether you're a novice or an experienced cook, Passover can result in hours spent hunting down recipes from friends and family or scrambling through piles of cookbooks. Now Passover cooking can become "a piece of cake" with the new book, *Passover Cookery: In the Kitchen with Joan Kekst.* You can create a new, distinctive feast or reproduce the beautiful traditions from your grandmother's Seder with Kekst's easy to follow steps and innovative recipes from her extensive private collection. From daily fare to gourmet, "kosher for Passover" delights have never been easier or more delicious! ISBN 1-877749-44-3

Household Careers: Nannies, Butlers, Maids & More: The Complete Guide for Finding Household Employment

By Linda F. Radke

Numerous professional positions are available in the child-care and home-help fields. This award-winning book provides all the information you need to find and secure a household job. ISBN 1-877749-05-2

Nannies, Maids & More: The Complete Guide for Hiring Household Help

By Linda F. Radke

Anyone who has had to hire household help knows what a challenge it can be. This book provides a step-by-step guide to hiring—and keeping—household help, complete with sample ads, interview questions, and employment forms. ISBN 0-9619853-2-1

Shoah: Journey From the Ashes

By Cantor Leo Fettman and Paul M. Howey

Cantor Leo Fettman survived the horrors of Auschwitz while millions of others, including almost his entire family, did not. He worked in the crematorium, was a victim of Dr. Josef Mengele's experiments, and lived through an attempted hanging by the SS. His remarkable tale of survival and subsequent joy is an inspiration for all. *Shoah* includes a historical prologue that chronicles the 2,000 years of anti-Semitism that led to the Holocaust. Cantor Fettman's message is one of love and hope, yet it contains an important warning for new generations to remember so the evils of the past will not be repeated. ISBN 0-9679721-0-8

Other Fine Titles From
Five Star Publications, Incorporated

Most titles are available through
www.BarnesandNoble.com and www.amazon.com

The Proper Pig's Guide to Mealtime Manners

By L.A. Kowal and Sally Starbuck Stamp

No one in your family would ever act like a pig at mealtime, but perhaps you know another family with that problem. This whimsical guide, complete with its own ceramic pig, gives valuable advice for children and adults alike on how to make mealtimes more fun and mannerly.
ISBN 1-877749-20-6

Junk Mail Solution

By Jackie Plusch

Jackie Plusch's Junk Mail Solution can help stop the aggravating intrusion of unwanted solicitations by both mail and phone. She offers three easy steps for freeing yourself from junk mailers and telemarketers. The book also includes pre-addressed cards to major mass marketing companies and handy script cards to put by your phones.
ISBN 0-9673136-1-9